Coco the Pug: A Pawsome Adventure

This is a work of fiction. Names, characters, businesses, organizations, places, events, and incidents either are the product of the author's imagination or are used fictitiously. Any resemblance to actual persons, living or dead, events, or locales is entirely coincidental.

The following trademarked terms are mentioned in this book: Mohamed El Afia. The use of these trademarks does not indicate an endorsement of this work by the trademark owners. The trademarks are used in a purely descriptive sense and all trademark rights remain with the trademark owner.

Cover design by el Emma afia.

This book was typeset in Emma afia.

First edition, 2023.

Published by Emma Afia.

Chapter 1: Coco's Missing Toy

- Introduction to Coco, an adorable and playful pug.
- Coco's favorite chew toy goes missing, causing Coco to feel sad.
- Coco sets out on a mission to find his beloved toy.
- Coco encounters some animal friends who offer to help him in his search.

Chapter 2: The Clues Unraveled

- Coco and his new friends begin searching for clues to find the missing toy.
- They explore Coco's favorite places, like the park and the backyard.
- Coco's sharp sense of smell leads them to discover some intriguing clues.
- The group starts piecing together the puzzle and gets closer to finding the toy.

Chapter 3: A Mischievous Adventure

- Coco and his friends follow a trail of clues that takes them on a mischievous adventure.
- They encounter obstacles and face funny and unexpected challenges along the way.
- Coco's determination and clever thinking help the group overcome the obstacles.
- Their adventure brings them closer together and strengthens their friendship.

Chapter 4: Lessons Learned

- Coco and his friends finally locate the missing toy in an unexpected place.
- They realize that it was accidentally hidden during a game they played.
- Coco learns the importance of being careful with his belongings.
- The group reflects on the adventures they had and the lessons they learned.

Chapter 5: Happy Reunion

- Coco is overjoyed to have his toy back, and he thanks his friends for their help.
- They celebrate their successful mission with a joyful gathering.
- Coco realizes that true friendship and teamwork made the adventure unforgettable.
- The story ends on a heartwarming note as Coco and his friends continue their adventures together.

Chapter 1: Coco's Missing Toy

Coco was a cute and energetic pug who loved to play with his favorite chew toy. The toy was his constant companion, and he carried it with him everywhere he went. One day, Coco realized that his beloved toy was missing. He searched all around the house and yard but couldn't find it anywhere. Coco became sad and worried that he might never find his toy again.

Determined to find his missing toy, Coco set out on a mission. He wandered around the house and yard, sniffing and searching for any clues. Suddenly, Coco noticed some strange marks on the ground that looked like paw prints. He followed the trail of paw prints and found himself at the edge of the yard.

Coco was hesitant to leave the safety of his yard, but he was determined to find his toy. As he ventured out, he met some new animal friends who offered to help him in his search. Coco was thrilled to have the help, and together they set out on a quest to find the missing toy.

As they searched, Coco's animal friends asked him to describe the toy's appearance and the places he had been playing. They tried to gather as much information as possible to help them find the toy. Coco was excited that he had some new friends to play with, but he was also worried that they might not be able to find his toy. Nonetheless, he remained optimistic that they would succeed in their mission.

Chapter 2: The Clues Unraveled

Coco and his newfound animal friends embarked on their search for Coco's missing toy. They started by retracing Coco's steps, visiting all his favorite places. They went to the park where Coco loved to chase squirrels and roll around in the grass. They searched the backyard where Coco enjoyed digging holes and sunbathing. Everywhere they went, they carefully examined the surroundings, hoping to spot a clue.

Coco's sharp sense of smell came in handy as they scoured the areas. He sniffed the air and followed his instincts, leading the group to some intriguing discoveries. They found a chewed-up stick that resembled Coco's toy, but it turned out to be a false alarm. However, they didn't lose hope and continued their search with determination.

As they explored further, Coco's friends noticed a pattern in the clues they found. They realized that Coco's toy had likely been taken during a playful game they had all participated in. They started piecing together the puzzle, connecting the dots, and unraveling the mystery behind the missing toy. Excitement filled the air as they drew closer to finding it.

With each clue they found, Coco's confidence grew. He felt grateful for the support of his friends, who cheered him on throughout the search. Coco learned that teamwork and collaboration were essential in solving problems and achieving goals. And so, they pressed on, eager to uncover the final clue that would lead them to Coco's beloved toy.

Chapter 3: A Mischievous Adventure

Armed with the clues they had gathered, Coco and his friends embarked on a thrilling and mischievous adventure. The trail led them to a nearby forest, where they encountered tall trees, rustling leaves, and a sense of excitement in the air. As they ventured deeper into the woods, they faced funny and unexpected challenges that tested their problem-solving skills. Coco's determination and quick thinking proved to be invaluable. He used his small size to squeeze through tight spaces and sniff out hidden objects. His friends cheered him on and followed his lead, providing encouragement and assistance along the way. They laughed and played, turning their search into an exciting game of exploration.

Their mischievous adventure took them through a maze of fallen logs, a bubbling brook they had to cross, and even a treehouse perched high above the ground. Coco and his friends giggled and squealed with delight as they swung from branches and slid down ropes. The forest became their playground, and their bond grew stronger with each shared adventure.

As they overcame each challenge, Coco and his friends felt a sense of accomplishment. They realized that even though the search for Coco's toy was important, the real treasure lay in the memories they were creating together. Their mischievous adventure taught them to appreciate the joy of the journey and the laughter shared along the way. Little did they know that their greatest reward was just around the corner.

Chapter 4: Lessons Learned

After their eventful and mischievous adventure in the forest, Coco and his friends finally arrived at a clearing where they discovered the missing toy. It had been hidden during their game, and they hadn't realized it at the time. Coco felt a mix of relief and happiness as he held his beloved toy once again.

As they gathered around the toy, Coco and his friends reflected on their journey and the lessons they had learned. They realized the importance of being careful with their belongings and how easily things can get misplaced or lost. Coco understood that he should cherish his toy and keep it in a safe place when not playing with it.

The group also learned about the power of friendship and teamwork. Coco's friends expressed how much they enjoyed joining him in the search for his toy. They emphasized that working together, sharing ideas, and supporting one another made the adventure more enjoyable and fruitful.

Coco felt grateful for their help and understood the value of relying on others when facing challenges.

With a renewed sense of gratitude and responsibility, Coco and his friends made a promise to always look out for one another. They pledged to be more mindful and organized, ensuring that they would not lose or misplace things in the future. Their shared experience had taught them important life lessons, and their bond grew even stronger as a result.

Chapter 5: Happy Reunion

Filled with joy and a sense of accomplishment, Coco and his friends celebrated their successful mission. They gathered together in Coco's backyard, surrounded by laughter, smiles, and wagging tails. The atmosphere was full of excitement as they relished in the happy reunion with Coco's beloved toy.

Coco couldn't contain his gratitude and appreciation for his friends. He thanked them for their unwavering support, their clever ideas, and their willingness to join him on this adventure. Coco's friends, in turn, expressed how much they cherished the friendship they had developed and how proud they were of Coco's determination.

To commemorate their journey and the bond they had formed, Coco's friends surprised him with a special gift. They presented him with a personalized collar that had a small charm shaped like Coco's toy. Coco's eyes sparkled with delight as he proudly wore the collar around his neck, a constant reminder of the unforgettable adventure they had shared.

As the day came to an end, Coco and his friends sat together, reflecting on their incredible journey. They realized that true friendship goes beyond material possessions and extends to the memories and experiences shared. Coco understood that he had found something far more precious than his toy – he had found lifelong friends who would always be by his side.

With hearts full of love and gratitude, Coco and his friends embraced the future, excited for the new adventures that awaited them. As the sun set, they bid farewell, knowing that their bond would forever be cherished and that the memories of their pawsome adventure would live on in their hearts.

The End

This is a work of fiction. Names, characters, businesses, organizations, places, events, and incidents either are the product of the author's imagination or are used fictitiously. Any resemblance to actual persons, living or dead, events, or locales is entirely coincidental.

The following trademarked terms are mentioned in this book: Mohamed El Afia. The use of these trademarks does not indicate an endorsement of this work by the trademark owners. The trademarks are used in a purely descriptive sense and all trademark rights remain with the trademark owner.

Cover design by el Emma afia.

This book was typeset in Emma afia.

First edition, 2023.

Published by Emma Afia.

Made in the USA
Monee, IL
17 December 2023

49447614R00015